Twisted Love; Horizons

Twisted Love, Volume 2

Mrigendra Bharti

Published by Sellbrochure Vymish Entertainment, 2024.

This is a work of fiction. Similarities to real people, places, or events are entirely coincidental.

TWISTED LOVE; HORIZONS

First edition. June 15, 2024.

ISBN: 979-8227388261

Written by Mrigendra Bharti.

Table of Contents

Preface:

Welcome to the world of Twisted Love: Horizons. In this captivating continuation of Aarushi's journey, we delve deeper into the complexities of love, friendship, and self-discovery.

As we rejoin Aarushi on her path, we witness her navigating through uncharted territories, facing unforeseen challenges, and embracing the endless possibilities that lie on the horizon. Each page is filled with moments of joy, sorrow, and revelation, as Aarushi learns valuable lessons about resilience, forgiveness, and the enduring power of love.

Twisted Love: Horizons is not just a story; it's a journey of growth and transformation, of highs and lows, of heartache and hope. It's a reminder that life is a series of twists and turns, and that sometimes, the most unexpected paths lead to the most beautiful destinations.

So, dear reader, fasten your seatbelt and prepare to embark on a journey like no other. Let the winds of fate guide you as we explore the vast horizons of love, loss, and everything in between.

Prologue:

In the quiet halls of memory, where echoes of the past linger like whispers in the wind, there lies a tale of love and loss, of shattered dreams and second chances. It is a story that unfolds in the hearts of those who dare to love fiercely, to dream boldly, and to brave the stormy seas of the human soul.

Our journey begins in a world much like our own, where the sun rises and sets on hopes and fears, where destiny weaves its intricate tapestry of fate. Here, amidst the bustling corridors of high school, we find our protagonist, Aarushi, a young girl on the cusp of womanhood, grappling with the complexities of love and friendship.

But beneath the surface of Aarushi's seemingly ordinary life lies a web of secrets and desires, of longing and regret. For Aarushi is not just another face in the crowd; she is a soul in search of truth, a heart yearning for redemption.

As we embark on this journey together, let us heed the call of adventure, of discovery, of the unknown. For in the pages that follow, we will witness the triumphs and tribulations of the human spirit, the joys and sorrows of love's enduring quest.

So, dear reader, cast aside your doubts and fears, and let us delve into the depths of Twisted Love: Horizons, where every twist and turn leads us closer to the truth, and every horizon promises a new beginning.

Acknowledgment:

To those who have embarked on their own journey of love and self-discovery, facing the twists and turns of life with courage and grace. Your stories have inspired and shaped the narrative of Twisted Love: Horizons, reminding us that the human spirit is resilient, and that even in the darkest of times, there is always light to guide us.

Introduction:

Welcome to the world of Twisted Love: Horizons, where the boundaries of the heart are tested, and the journey of self-discovery knows no bounds. In this captivating continuation of Aarushi's story, we delve deeper into the complexities of love, friendship, and the human spirit.

As we rejoin Aarushi on her journey, we find her standing at the crossroads of her past and her future, grappling with the aftermath of heartache and betrayal, and seeking solace in the promise of new beginnings. But the path ahead is anything but certain, as Aarushi navigates through uncharted territories of emotion, facing unforeseen challenges and embracing the boundless possibilities that lie on the horizon.

In the pages that follow, you will witness the triumphs and tribulations of a young woman on a quest for truth and redemption, as she learns valuable lessons about resilience, forgiveness, and the enduring power of love. You will accompany Aarushi on a journey of self-discovery, as she explores the depths of her own heart and discovers the strength within herself to overcome any obstacle that stands in her way.

Twisted Love: Horizons is more than just a story; it is a testament to the resilience of the human spirit, a celebration of the beauty and complexity of the human experience, and a reminder that even in the darkest of times, there is always hope on the horizon.

So, dear reader, prepare to embark on a journey like no other, as we delve into the depths of the human soul and discover the true meaning of love, loss, and everything in between.

Connect With Mrigendra,
Thank you very much for choosing this book.
You can also connect with me on Instagram,
https://www.instagram.com/i_mrigendrabharti.official
With Love,
Mrigendra Bharti

Chapter 6: A New Beginning

Part 1: Unexpected Encounters

The crisp autumn air hung heavy with the promise of change as Aarushi made her way through the bustling corridors of her school. The familiar chatter of students echoed in her ears, but today, there was a sense of anticipation tingling in the air, as if something new and exciting was on the horizon.

Lost in her thoughts, Aarushi rounded a corner and collided with someone, nearly sending her books flying to the ground. With a gasp of surprise, she looked up to see a boy standing before her, a sheepish grin on his face.

"I'm so sorry," he exclaimed, reaching out to steady her. "I wasn't watching where I was going."

Aarushi couldn't help but smile at his earnestness, feeling a spark of curiosity ignite within her. She studied the boy before her, taking in his tousled hair and mischievous eyes, and felt a strange sense of familiarity wash over her.

"It's alright," she replied, her voice soft with amusement. "No harm done."

As they exchanged introductions, Aarushi felt a sense of warmth and camaraderie blooming between them. She learned that his name was Kabir, a new student at the school, and that he had recently moved to the area with his family.

As they parted ways, Aarushi couldn't shake off the feeling of intrigue that lingered within her. There was something about Kabir that drew her in, something magnetic and irresistible that she couldn't quite put into words.

With a smile playing on her lips, Aarushi continued on her way, her heart brimming with excitement at the prospect of new friendships and unexpected encounters that lay ahead.

Part 2: The Bonding Begins

As days turned into weeks, Aarushi found herself drawn to Kabir's infectious energy and zest for life. Their chance encounter had blossomed into a budding friendship, one filled with laughter, shared interests, and mutual understanding.

During lunch breaks and after school, Aarushi and Kabir would often find themselves engrossed in deep conversations, discussing everything from their favorite books to their dreams for the future. There was a comfort in their companionship, a sense of belonging that Aarushi hadn't felt in a long time.

Despite the chaos of her own life, Aarushi found solace in Kabir's presence. He was a breath of fresh air amidst the turmoil of her thoughts, a reminder that amidst the darkness, there was still light to be found.

As they walked home together one afternoon, Aarushi couldn't help but marvel at the bond that had formed between them. It was as if they had known each other for years, their connection deep and unshakeable.

With a smile tugging at her lips, Aarushi realized that in Kabir, she had found not just a friend, but a kindred spirit, someone who understood her in a way no one else did. And as they continued on their journey together, she knew that no matter what the future held, they would face it side by side, with courage, laughter, and an unwavering belief in the power of their friendship.

Part 3: Unveiling Truths

The days melted into weeks, and Aarushi found herself immersed in the warmth of her newfound friendship with Kabir. They spent their afternoons exploring the nooks and crannies of their small town, chasing after sunsets and sharing secrets beneath the starlit sky.

Yet, amidst the laughter and camaraderie, a nagging sense of unease gnawed at the edges of Aarushi's mind. She couldn't shake off the feeling that something was amiss, something lurking in the shadows, waiting to be unveiled.

One fateful afternoon, as Aarushi and Kabir wandered through the town square, they stumbled upon an old bookstore tucked away in a forgotten corner. Intrigued by the promise of hidden treasures, they stepped inside, the musty scent of old books enveloping them like a comforting embrace.

As they browsed through the shelves, Aarushi's eyes fell upon a weathered leather-bound journal nestled amongst the stacks. Intrigued, she reached out and traced her fingers along its faded cover, a sense of curiosity stirring within her.

"Look what I found," she exclaimed, holding up the journal for Kabir to see. "Isn't it fascinating?"

Kabir's eyes lit up with excitement as he took the journal from her hands, flipping through its yellowed pages with eager anticipation. "It's like stepping back in time," he mused, his voice filled with wonder.

As they delved deeper into the journal's contents, Aarushi felt a sense of familiarity wash over her. There, amidst the scribbled notes and faded ink, were glimpses of a world long forgotten, a world that bore striking similarities to her own.

But as they reached the final pages of the journal, Aarushi's heart skipped a beat as she stumbled upon a revelation that sent shockwaves through her soul. There, in black and white, were the words she had been dreading to see, the truth she had been afraid to confront.

As Kabir read aloud the final entry, Aarushi felt the ground shift beneath her feet, her world tilting on its axis as she grappled with the enormity of what she had uncovered. The journal held the key to a long-buried secret, a secret that threatened to unravel the very fabric of her existence.

With trembling hands, Aarushi closed the journal, her mind swirling with a whirlwind of emotions. She knew that she couldn't keep the truth hidden any longer, that she had to confront the ghosts of her past and lay them to rest once and for all.

As they left the bookstore behind and made their way home, Aarushi felt a sense of determination coursing through her veins. She knew that the road ahead would be fraught with challenges and uncertainties, but she also knew that she couldn't turn back now.

With Kabir by her side, she would face the truth head-on, no matter where it led her. For she was done running from her demons, done hiding from the darkness that threatened to consume her.

As the sun dipped below the horizon, casting a golden glow across the sky, Aarushi took a deep breath and stepped into the unknown, ready to embrace whatever the future held, armed with nothing but courage, resilience, and the unwavering belief that the truth would set her free.

Part 4: Embracing the Truth

As the sun dipped below the horizon, casting a warm glow over the sleepy town, Aarushi found herself standing at the crossroads of her past and her future. With Kabir by her side, she had unraveled the secrets buried within the pages of the old journal, confronting the truth head-on with courage and resilience.

But as she stared out into the fading light, Aarushi knew that her journey was far from over. There were still unanswered questions lingering in the air, still mysteries waiting to be solved. And though the path ahead was shrouded in darkness, she knew that she couldn't turn back now.

With a determined set to her jaw, Aarushi took Kabir's hand in hers, drawing strength from his unwavering presence. Together, they set off into the night, their footsteps echoing in the silence as they ventured into the unknown.

As they walked, Aarushi couldn't shake off the feeling of anticipation that tingled in the air. She knew that whatever lay ahead would test her in ways she couldn't imagine, but she also knew that she was ready to face it with courage and determination.

With each step forward, Aarushi felt a sense of clarity wash over her, a clarity born from the knowledge that she was finally free from the shackles of her past. She had confronted her demons, laid them to rest, and now, she was ready to embrace the future with open arms.

As they reached the edge of town, Aarushi paused, her heart heavy with the weight of the journey that lay ahead. But as she looked up at the stars twinkling in the night sky, she felt a sense of peace settle over her, a peace born from the knowledge that she was no longer alone.

With a smile playing on her lips, Aarushi turned to Kabir, her eyes shining with determination. "Thank you," she whispered, her voice barely above a whisper. "For everything."

Kabir returned her smile, his eyes alight with understanding. "Anytime," he replied, his voice soft with emotion. "I'll always be here for you, no matter what."

And with that, they set off into the night, their hearts filled with hope and possibility, their souls bound together by the unbreakable bonds of friendship and love.

Chapter 7: Heartfelt Confessions

Part 1: A Tangled Web

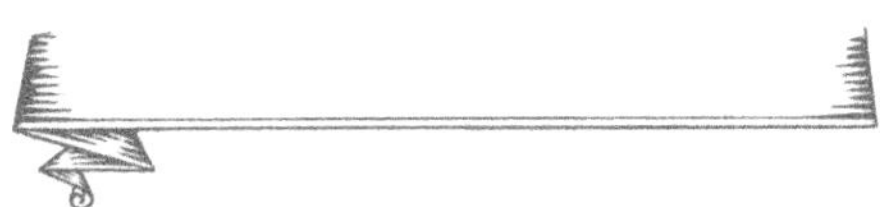

The sun rose over the horizon, casting a golden glow across the sleepy town as Aarushi stepped out into the crisp morning air. She couldn't shake off the events of the previous night, the revelations and emotions swirling in her mind like a tempestuous storm.

As she made her way through the familiar streets, Aarushi's thoughts turned to Kabir, the steadfast friend who had stood by her side through thick and thin. There was a comfort in his presence, a sense of solace that she couldn't find anywhere else.

But amidst the warmth of their friendship, there lingered a shadow of doubt, a nagging sense of unease that refused to be ignored. Aarushi couldn't help but wonder if there was more to their relationship than met the eye, if the feelings she harbored for Kabir ran deeper than mere friendship.

Lost in her thoughts, Aarushi found herself standing outside the school gates, her heart heavy with uncertainty. She knew that she couldn't keep her feelings bottled up inside forever, that she had to confront the truth and lay her cards on the table once and for all.

As she stepped into the bustling halls of the school, Aarushi's eyes scanned the crowd, searching for a familiar face amidst the sea of students. And there, amidst the throng of bodies, she spotted Kabir, his smile lighting up the room like a beacon of hope.

With a determined set to her jaw, Aarushi made her way towards him, her heart pounding in her chest with each step she took. She knew that she had to be honest with him, to lay bare the truth of her feelings and see where the chips fell.

"Hey," she greeted him, her voice tinged with nervousness. "Can we talk?"

Kabir turned to her, his eyes soft with concern. "Of course," he replied, his voice gentle. "What's on your mind?"

Taking a deep breath, Aarushi gathered her courage and spoke from the heart, laying bare the truth of her feelings for Kabir. She poured out her soul, confessing the depth of her emotions and the turmoil that had plagued her ever since they had met.

As she spoke, Aarushi watched as a myriad of emotions flickered across Kabir's face, from surprise to confusion to something else she couldn't quite place. And when she finally fell silent, she held her breath, waiting for his response with bated breath.

For a moment, there was silence between them, the air thick with tension as Kabir processed her words. And then, with a soft smile playing on his lips, he reached out and took her hand in his, his touch sending sparks flying through her veins.

"Aarushi," he began, his voice barely above a whisper. "I had no idea you felt this way."

Aarushi's heart skipped a beat at his words, her pulse quickening with anticipation. She held her breath, waiting for him to continue, her entire being hanging on his every word.

"But," Kabir continued, his expression serious. "There's something I need to tell you."

Aarushi's stomach clenched with apprehension as she waited for him to speak, her mind racing with a million possibilities. What could Kabir possibly have to say that would change everything between them?

With a deep breath, Kabir looked into her eyes, his gaze unwavering. "I have feelings for you too, Aarushi," he confessed, his voice raw with emotion. "But there's something you need to know before we go any further."

Aarushi's heart pounded in her chest as Kabir's words hung in the air, the weight of his confession settling over her like a heavy blanket. What could he possibly have to tell her that would change everything between them?

With a sinking feeling in the pit of her stomach, Aarushi braced herself for the truth, steeling herself for whatever revelation was about to come. Little did she know that the road ahead would be filled with twists and turns, revelations and betrayals, leading her down a path she never could have imagined.

But for now, all she could do was wait, her heart hanging in the balance as she prepared to face the truth head-on.

Part 2: Unraveling the Past

As Kabir's words hung in the air, Aarushi felt as though the ground had been pulled out from beneath her feet. She had braced herself for the truth, but nothing could have prepared her for what Kabir was about to reveal.

Taking a deep breath, Kabir looked into Aarushi's eyes, his expression pained. "There's something I haven't told you," he began, his voice tinged with regret. "Something that I should have shared with you from the beginning."

Aarushi's heart clenched with apprehension as she waited for him to continue, her mind racing with a million possibilities. What could Kabir possibly have to tell her that would change everything between them?

With a heavy sigh, Kabir launched into his confession, his words tumbling out in a rush as he laid bare the truth of his past. He spoke of a love lost, of a heartbroken soul searching for redemption, of mistakes made and lessons learned.

As he spoke, Aarushi listened in stunned silence, her mind reeling from the enormity of what Kabir was revealing. She had never imagined that his past could be so fraught with pain and sorrow, so filled with secrets and regrets.

But amidst the darkness, there was a glimmer of light, a beacon of hope that shone through the shadows. For Kabir spoke not just of his past, but of his present, of the love that had blossomed between them amidst the chaos of their lives.

And as she listened to his words, Aarushi felt a sense of clarity wash over her, a clarity born from the knowledge that she was not alone. Kabir may have his demons, his secrets, his regrets, but so did she. And together, they could face whatever the future held, armed with nothing but the strength of their love.

With tears in her eyes, Aarushi reached out and took Kabir's hand in hers, her heart overflowing with emotion. "Thank you for telling me," she whispered, her voice soft with gratitude. "I may not have all the answers, but I know that together, we can overcome anything."

And as they stood there, hand in hand, Aarushi felt a sense of peace settle over her, a peace born from the knowledge that no matter what the future held, they would face it together, with courage, resilience, and an unwavering belief in the power of their love.

Part 3: Embracing the Present

As the weight of Kabir's confession hung heavy in the air, Aarushi felt a whirlwind of emotions swirling within her. She had never imagined that their journey together would be marked by such profound revelations, such deep-seated truths.

But amidst the chaos, there was a sense of clarity, a sense of purpose that burned brightly within her heart. For Kabir had laid bare his soul before her, revealing the depths of his love and the sincerity of his intentions.

With a determined set to her jaw, Aarushi took a deep breath and spoke from the heart, laying bare her own fears and insecurities for Kabir to see. She spoke of the doubts that had plagued her, the uncertainties that had kept her awake at night, and the overwhelming sense of longing that had consumed her soul.

And as she spoke, she watched as Kabir's eyes softened with understanding, his gaze unwavering as he listened to her every word. There was a tenderness in his touch, a warmth in his embrace, that made Aarushi feel safe and cherished in a way she had never known before.

With tears in her eyes, Aarushi reached out and cupped Kabir's face in her hands, her heart overflowing with emotion. "I love you," she whispered, her voice barely above a whisper. "I love you more than words can say."

And as she spoke those three simple words, Aarushi felt a weight lift from her shoulders, a burden lifted from her soul. For in that moment, she knew that she had found what she had been searching for all along – a love that was pure, a love that was true, a love that would stand the test of time.

With a smile playing on her lips, Aarushi leaned in and pressed her lips to Kabir's, sealing their love with a kiss that spoke volumes more than words ever could. And as they stood there, wrapped in each other's arms, Aarushi felt a sense of peace settle over her, a peace born from the knowledge that she had finally found her home in the arms of the man she loved.

Part 4: The Path Forward

As the sun dipped below the horizon, casting a warm glow over the sleepy town, Aarushi and Kabir found themselves lost in each other's arms, their hearts beating as one. They had laid bare their souls before each other, baring their deepest fears and insecurities, and in the process, had forged a bond that was unbreakable.

But amidst the warmth of their embrace, there lingered a sense of uncertainty, a nagging doubt that refused to be ignored. For Aarushi knew that their journey together was far from over, that the road ahead would be fraught with challenges and obstacles that they would have to overcome together.

With a heavy sigh, Aarushi pulled away from Kabir's embrace, her heart heavy with the weight of the future that lay before them. "What do we do now?" she asked, her voice tinged with uncertainty.

Kabir reached out and took her hand in his, his touch sending shivers down her spine. "We take it one step at a time," he replied, his voice steady and reassuring. "Together."

And with that simple declaration, Aarushi felt a sense of peace settle over her, a sense of clarity that she hadn't felt in a long time. For in Kabir's eyes, she saw a reflection of her own hopes and dreams, a promise of a future filled with love and happiness.

As they walked hand in hand through the quiet streets, Aarushi felt a sense of gratitude wash over her, a gratitude for the man who had come into her life and changed it in ways she could never have imagined. With each step they took, she felt a renewed sense of purpose, a renewed determination to face whatever challenges lay ahead with courage and resilience.

As they reached the edge of town, Aarushi and Kabir paused, their eyes locked in a silent exchange of understanding. They knew that the road ahead would be difficult, that there would be obstacles and setbacks along the way, but they also knew that as long as they had each other, they could overcome anything.

With a smile playing on her lips, Aarushi turned to Kabir, her heart overflowing with love and gratitude. "Thank you," she whispered, her voice barely above a whisper. "For everything."

Kabir returned her smile, his eyes shining with love and affection. "Anytime," he replied, his voice soft with emotion. "I'll always be here for you, no matter what."

And with that simple declaration of love, Aarushi and Kabir stepped into the unknown, their hearts entwined as they faced the future together, hand in hand, with courage, resilience, and an unwavering belief in the power of their love.

Chapter 8: New Horizons

Part 1: A Fresh Start

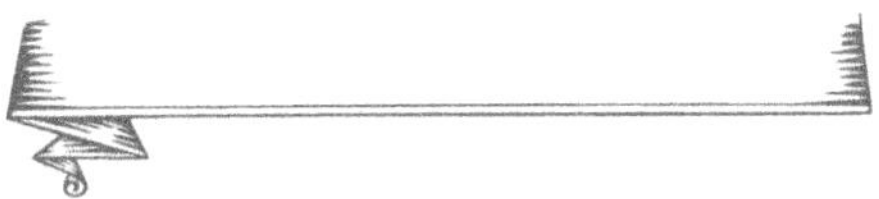

As the sun rose over the horizon, painting the sky in hues of pink and gold, Aarushi stood at the threshold of a new beginning. The events of the past had shaped her in ways she could never have imagined, but now, as she looked to the future, she felt a sense of excitement tinged with apprehension.

With Kabir by her side, Aarushi embarked on the journey of rebuilding her life, one step at a time. Together, they faced each day with courage and resilience, determined to carve out a future filled with love and happiness.

Their days were filled with laughter and joy, as they explored the world around them with a sense of wonder and curiosity. They visited quaint cafes and bustling markets, hiked through verdant forests and climbed to the tops of towering mountains, each adventure bringing them closer together.

But amidst the beauty of their surroundings, there lingered a sense of unease, a feeling that they were being watched, that danger lurked just beyond the horizon. Aarushi couldn't shake off the feeling that their past was catching up with them, that they were not as safe as they seemed.

One fateful afternoon, as they wandered through the heart of the city, Aarushi's fears were realized as they found themselves face to face with a figure from their past. It was Rahul, the boy who had once held her heart in his hands, his eyes filled with anger and resentment.

Aarushi's heart pounded in her chest as she watched Rahul approach, her mind racing with a million thoughts. She had thought that she had left her past behind her, that she had moved on from the pain and heartache that had once consumed her. But now, as Rahul stood before her, she realized that the past was not so easily forgotten.

With a heavy heart, Aarushi turned to Kabir, her eyes filled with uncertainty. She didn't know how to face Rahul, how to confront the demons of her past. But Kabir was there, his presence a steady anchor in the stormy sea of her emotions.

Together, they stood tall, facing Rahul with courage and determination. They listened as he poured out his heart, his words filled with regret and remorse. He spoke of his own struggles, his own demons, and the pain that had haunted him ever since they had parted ways.

And as Aarushi listened, she felt a sense of empathy wash over her, a recognition of the shared humanity that bound them together. For in Rahul's words, she saw a reflection of her own pain, her own longing for redemption.

With a heavy heart, Aarushi reached out and took Rahul's hand in hers, her eyes filled with compassion. "I forgive you," she whispered, her voice barely above a whisper. "For everything."

And as she spoke those words, Aarushi felt a weight lift from her shoulders, a burden lifted from her soul. For in forgiveness, she found peace, a peace born from the knowledge that she had finally let go of the past and embraced the future with open arms.

With Rahul by their side, Aarushi and Kabir embarked on a new chapter of their lives, one filled with hope and promise.

They knew that the road ahead would be difficult, that there would be challenges and obstacles to overcome, but they also knew that as long as they had each other, they could face anything that came their way.

As the sun dipped below the horizon, casting a warm glow over the city, Aarushi looked to the future with renewed optimism. She didn't know what lay ahead, but she knew that as long as she had Kabir by her side, she could face whatever came her way with courage, resilience, and an unwavering belief in the power of love.

And so, hand in hand, they walked into the unknown, their hearts filled with hope and their souls ablaze with the promise of a new beginning.

Part 2: Facing Challenges

As Aarushi and Kabir ventured further into their new chapter, they encountered challenges that tested the strength of their bond and the depth of their love. Despite their determination to leave the past behind, its echoes continued to reverberate, threatening to disrupt the fragile peace they had found.

One such challenge arose when they stumbled upon Sameer, Aarushi's childhood friend, on a quiet afternoon stroll through the park. His presence caught them off guard, stirring up memories of a time long gone and emotions they had buried deep within.

Sameer's eyes lit up with surprise and delight as he spotted Aarushi and Kabir, his smile warm and genuine. He approached them with open arms, eager to reconnect with his old friend and meet the person who had captured her heart.

Aarushi's heart swelled with nostalgia as she embraced Sameer, her mind flooded with memories of their shared childhood adventures. But beneath the surface, a sense of unease simmered, a reminder of the secrets she had kept hidden from him for so long.

As they exchanged pleasantries, Aarushi felt the weight of her silence pressing down on her, a burden she could no longer bear. She knew that she had to come clean, to lay bare the truth of her past and face the consequences, whatever they may be.

With a heavy heart, Aarushi turned to Sameer, her eyes filled with apprehension. "There's something I need to tell you," she began, her voice trembling with emotion. "Something I should have told you a long time ago."

Sameer's brow furrowed with concern as he listened to her words, his eyes searching hers for answers. He could sense the gravity of what she was about to reveal, the weight of the secrets she had carried with her for so long.

And as Aarushi spoke, laying bare the truth of her past and the depths of her love for Kabir, Sameer listened in stunned silence, his mind reeling from the enormity of what he was hearing. He had never imagined that Aarushi's life could be so complicated, so fraught with pain and heartache.

But amidst the chaos of their emotions, there was a glimmer of hope, a promise of redemption that beckoned them forward. For in the honesty of Aarushi's confession, Sameer saw the strength of her character, the depth of her love, and the resilience of her spirit.

With tears in his eyes, Sameer reached out and took Aarushi's hand in his, his grip firm and reassuring. "Thank you for telling me," he whispered, his voice filled with emotion. "I may not understand everything, but I'll always be here for you, no matter what."

And as they stood there, united by the bonds of friendship and love, Aarushi felt a sense of peace settle over her, a peace born from the knowledge that she was no longer alone. With Sameer by her side, she knew that she could face whatever challenges lay ahead with courage, resilience, and an unwavering belief in the power of love.

As they parted ways, Aarushi and Kabir walked hand in hand through the park, their hearts filled with gratitude and hope. They knew that the road ahead would be difficult, that there would be obstacles and setbacks along the way, but they also knew that as long as they had each other, they could overcome anything that stood in their path.

And so, hand in hand, they walked into the future, their souls ablaze with the promise of a new beginning, a fresh start, and a love that would stand the test of time.

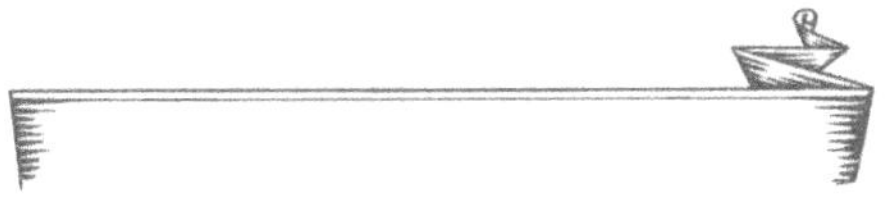

Part 3: Resilience and Growth

As Aarushi and Kabir navigated through the complexities of their past, they found themselves confronted with unexpected challenges that tested the strength of their bond and the resilience of their love. Each obstacle they faced served as a crucible, forging their relationship into something stronger, something more resilient.

One such challenge arose when they encountered Neha, an old acquaintance from their school days, during a chance encounter at a local coffee shop. Neha's presence stirred up memories of a time long gone, of friendships forged and broken, and of secrets buried beneath the surface.

As they exchanged pleasantries, Aarushi couldn't shake off the feeling of unease that gnawed at the edges of her mind. She knew that Neha was aware of the tumultuous events that had unfolded in their lives, and she couldn't help but wonder what secrets lay hidden behind her seemingly friendly facade.

As they sat sipping their coffee, Neha broached the topic of their shared past, her eyes alight with curiosity. She probed gently, asking questions that touched upon the events that had shaped their lives in ways they could never have imagined.

Aarushi felt a sense of apprehension building within her, a fear of the truths that lay buried beneath the surface. She knew that she couldn't keep her secrets hidden forever, that she had to confront the demons of her past and lay them to rest once and for all.

With a heavy heart, Aarushi took a deep breath and spoke from the heart, laying bare the truth of her past and the depths of her love for Kabir. She spoke of the pain and heartache that had haunted her for so long, of the struggles she had faced and the demons she had overcome.

As she spoke, Neha listened in stunned silence, her eyes wide with shock and disbelief. She had never imagined that Aarushi's life could be so complicated, so fraught with pain and sorrow. But amidst the chaos of their emotions, there was a glimmer of understanding, a recognition of the shared humanity that bound them together.

With tears in her eyes, Neha reached out and took Aarushi's hand in hers, her grip firm and reassuring. "Thank you for telling me," she whispered, her voice filled with emotion. "I may not understand everything, but I'll always be here for you, no matter what."

And as they sat there, united by the bonds of friendship and love, Aarushi felt a sense of peace settle over her, a peace born from the knowledge that she was no longer alone. With Neha by her side, she knew that she could face whatever challenges lay ahead with courage, resilience, and an unwavering belief in the power of love.

As they parted ways, Aarushi and Kabir walked hand in hand through the bustling streets, their hearts filled with gratitude and hope. They knew that the road ahead would be difficult, that there would be obstacles and setbacks along the way, but they also knew that as long as they had each other, they could overcome anything that stood in their path.

And so, hand in hand, they walked into the future, their souls ablaze with the promise of a new beginning, a fresh start, and a love that would stand the test of time.

Part 4: Embracing the Future

As Aarushi and Kabir continued on their journey of self-discovery and growth, they found themselves facing their final challenge, one that would test the strength of their resolve and the depth of their love.

It was a warm summer evening when they received an unexpected visitor at their doorstep. It was Aditi, Aarushi's estranged sister, whose presence brought with it a flood of memories and emotions that threatened to overwhelm them both.

Aditi's eyes brimmed with tears as she poured out her heart, confessing the pain and regret that had haunted her ever since they had parted ways. She spoke of her longing for reconciliation, her desire to mend the broken bonds that had torn their family apart.

Aarushi listened in stunned silence, her heart aching with the weight of Aditi's words. She had spent years nursing her wounds, nursing her anger and resentment towards her sister, but now, as she looked into Aditi's eyes, she saw nothing but a reflection of her own pain and longing for redemption.

With a heavy heart, Aarushi reached out and took Aditi's hand in hers, her grip firm and reassuring. "I forgive you," she whispered, her voice barely above a whisper. "For everything."

And as she spoke those words, Aarushi felt a sense of peace settle over her, a peace born from the knowledge that she had finally let go of the past and embraced the future with open arms.

Aditi's eyes filled with tears of gratitude as she embraced her sister, her heart overflowing with emotion. "Thank you," she whispered, her voice choked with emotion. "I promise to make things right, to earn back your trust and love."

And as they stood there, united by the bonds of family and love, Aarushi felt a sense of closure wash over her, a sense of healing that she hadn't felt in years. With Aditi by her side, she knew that she could face whatever challenges lay ahead with courage, resilience, and an unwavering belief in the power of love.

As they parted ways, Aarushi and Kabir watched as Aditi disappeared into the night, her heart filled with hope and promise. They knew that the road ahead would be difficult, that there would be obstacles and setbacks along the way, but they also knew that as long as they had each other, they could overcome anything that stood in their path.

And so, hand in hand, they walked into the future, their souls ablaze with the promise of a new beginning, a fresh start, and a love that would stand the test of time.

Chapter 9: Boundless Possibilities

Part 1: Discoveries and Revelations

As Aarushi and Kabir embarked on the next phase of their journey, they found themselves immersed in a whirlwind of new experiences and revelations. Each day brought with it the promise of boundless possibilities, as they explored the depths of their love and the world around them.

Their adventures took them to far-flung corners of the globe, from the bustling streets of Paris to the serene beaches of Bali. They immersed themselves in the rich tapestry of cultures and traditions, savoring each moment as if it were their last.

But amidst the beauty of their surroundings, there lingered a sense of unease, a feeling that they were being watched, that danger lurked just beyond the horizon. Aarushi couldn't shake off the feeling that their past was catching up with them, that they were not as safe as they seemed.

One fateful evening, as they wandered through the narrow alleyways of a quaint seaside town, Aarushi's fears were realized as they found themselves face to face with a figure from their past. It was Rohan, a childhood friend who had once held a special place in Aarushi's heart, his eyes filled with anger and resentment.

Aarushi's heart skipped a beat as she watched Rohan approach, her mind racing with a million thoughts. She had thought that she had left her past behind her, that she had moved on from the pain and heartache that had once consumed her. But now, as Rohan stood before her, she realized that the past was not so easily forgotten.

With a heavy heart, Aarushi turned to Kabir, her eyes filled with uncertainty. She didn't know how to face Rohan, how to confront the demons of her past. But Kabir was there, his presence a steady anchor in the stormy sea of her emotions.

Together, they stood tall, facing Rohan with courage and determination. They listened as he poured out his heart, his words filled with regret and remorse. He spoke of his own struggles, his own demons, and the pain that had haunted him ever since they had parted ways.

As he spoke, Aarushi listened in stunned silence, her mind reeling from the enormity of what she was hearing. She had never imagined that Rohan's life could be so complicated, so fraught with pain and sorrow. But amidst the chaos of their emotions, there was a glimmer of understanding, a recognition of the shared humanity that bound them together.

With tears in her eyes, Aarushi reached out and took Rohan's hand in hers, her grip firm and reassuring. "I forgive you," she whispered, her voice barely above a whisper. "For everything."

And as she spoke those words, Aarushi felt a weight lift from her shoulders, a burden lifted from her soul. For in forgiveness, she found peace, a peace born from the knowledge that she had finally let go of the past and embraced the future with open arms.

With Rohan by their side, Aarushi and Kabir embarked on a new chapter of their lives, one filled with hope and promise. They knew that the road ahead would be difficult, that there would be challenges and obstacles to overcome, but they also knew that as long as they had each other, they could face anything that came their way.

As the sun dipped below the horizon, casting a warm glow over the town, Aarushi looked to the future with renewed optimism. She didn't know what lay ahead, but she knew that as long as she had Kabir by her side, she could face whatever came her way with courage, resilience, and an unwavering belief in the power of love.

And so, hand in hand, they walked into the unknown, their hearts filled with hope and their souls ablaze with the promise of a new beginning, a fresh start, and a love that would stand the test of time.

Part 2: Unraveling the Past

As Aarushi and Kabir continued their journey, they found themselves drawn deeper into the mysteries of their past, uncovering secrets long buried and truths waiting to be revealed.

Their travels took them to remote corners of the world, where they immersed themselves in the beauty of nature and the richness of different cultures. But no matter how far they ventured, they couldn't escape the shadows of their past, which followed them like silent specters, haunting their every step.

One day, while exploring the ancient ruins of a forgotten civilization, they stumbled upon a hidden chamber buried deep beneath the earth. Intrigued by the discovery, they ventured inside, their hearts pounding with excitement and trepidation.

As they explored the chamber, they came across a series of ancient artifacts, each one shrouded in mystery and intrigue. Among them was a dusty old journal, its pages yellowed with age and its ink faded with time.

With trembling hands, Aarushi opened the journal and began to read, her heart racing as she delved into the secrets of the past. The journal belonged to a young woman named Maya, who had lived centuries ago during the time of the ancient civilization.

As Aarushi read Maya's words, she was transported back in time to a world long forgotten, a world filled with love, betrayal, and the relentless march of time. Maya spoke of her forbidden love for a man from a rival tribe, a love that had torn her world apart and left her heartbroken and alone.

But amidst the pain and heartache, there was a glimmer of hope, a promise of redemption that beckoned her forward. For Maya had discovered a hidden truth, a truth that would change the course of her destiny and the destiny of those she loved.

With each passing page, Aarushi felt a sense of kinship with Maya, a recognition of the shared struggles and triumphs that bound them together across the ages. She saw herself reflected in Maya's words, her own journey mirrored in the pages of the ancient journal.

As she reached the final page, Aarushi felt a sense of closure wash over her, a sense of peace born from the knowledge that she was not alone. For in Maya's story, she found the strength to confront her own demons, to embrace the truth of her past, and to forge a new future filled with hope and possibility.

With tears in her eyes, Aarushi closed the journal and turned to Kabir, her heart overflowing with emotion. "We're not alone," she whispered, her voice filled with wonder. "Maya's story is our story, a tale of love and redemption that spans the ages."

And as they stood there, hand in hand, Aarushi felt a sense of gratitude wash over her, a gratitude for the journey they had undertaken together, and the love that had carried them through the darkest of times.

With renewed determination, Aarushi and Kabir left the chamber behind and stepped out into the light of day, their hearts light and their spirits soaring. For they knew that no matter what trials lay ahead, they would face them together, with courage, resilience, and an unwavering belief in the power of love.

And so, hand in hand, they walked into the future, their souls ablaze with the promise of a new beginning, a fresh start, and a love that would stand the test of time.

Part 3: Navigating Challenges

As Aarushi and Kabir ventured further into their journey, they encountered obstacles that tested the strength of their bond and the resilience of their love. Yet, with each challenge they faced, they emerged stronger and more united than ever before.

One day, while exploring a remote mountain village nestled among the clouds, they found themselves caught in the midst of a sudden storm. The wind howled and the rain poured down, obscuring their path and threatening to sweep them away.

But amidst the chaos of the storm, there was a glimmer of hope, a beacon of light that guided them through the darkness. For Aarushi and Kabir knew that as long as they had each other, they could weather any storm that came their way.

With determination in their hearts, they pressed on, their hands tightly clasped together as they navigated the treacherous terrain. They slipped and stumbled, their clothes soaked through and their bodies battered by the elements, but they refused to give up.

As they reached the summit of the mountain, the storm began to recede, leaving behind a breathtaking vista of endless skies and rolling hills. A sense of peace washed over them, a peace born from the knowledge that they had conquered their fears and emerged victorious.

With the sun shining down upon them, Aarushi and Kabir shared a moment of quiet reflection, their hearts filled with gratitude for the journey they had undertaken together. They knew that the road ahead would be difficult, that there would be challenges and obstacles to overcome, but they also knew that as long as they had each other, they could face anything that came their way.

As they descended from the mountain and made their way back to civilization, Aarushi and Kabir felt a sense of renewal wash over them, a renewal born from the knowledge that their love was stronger than any storm. Hand in hand, they walked through the verdant valleys and meandering streams, their hearts filled with hope and their souls ablaze with the promise of a future filled with boundless possibilities.

And so, with each step they took, they embraced the challenges that lay ahead with open arms, knowing that together, they could conquer the world.

Part 4: Embracing the Future

As Aarushi and Kabir journeyed further into the unknown, they found themselves standing at the precipice of a new beginning, a future filled with endless possibilities and untold adventures. Despite the trials they had faced and the challenges they had overcome, their love remained steadfast, a beacon of hope that guided them through the darkest of times.

One evening, as they sat beneath a blanket of stars, their hearts heavy with the weight of the world, they found themselves contemplating the path that lay ahead. They knew that the road would not be easy, that there would be obstacles and setbacks along the way, but they also knew that as long as they had each other, they could face whatever came their way with courage and determination.

With renewed resolve, they made a pact to embrace the future with open arms, to seize each moment with passion and purpose, and to never lose sight of the love that had brought them together. They vowed to support each other through thick and thin, to lift each other up when they stumbled, and to celebrate each victory, no matter how small.

And so, as they watched the stars twinkle in the night sky, Aarushi and Kabir felt a sense of peace settle over them, a peace born from the knowledge that they were exactly where they were meant to be. Hand in hand, they looked to the future with hope and anticipation, their hearts filled with gratitude for the journey they had undertaken together.

As they drifted off to sleep beneath the canopy of stars, they knew that no matter what the future held, they would face it together, with love as their guiding light and each other as their constant companion. And as they dreamed of the adventures that lay ahead, their souls ablaze with the promise of a future filled with boundless possibilities, they knew that their love would endure for all eternity.

And so, with hearts full of hope and eyes shining bright, Aarushi and Kabir embarked on the next chapter of their journey, ready to embrace whatever the future had in store.

Chapter 10: Eternal Love

Part 1: A New Beginning

As Aarushi and Kabir embarked on the final chapter of their journey, they found themselves standing on the threshold of a new beginning, a future filled with endless possibilities and infinite love. Their hearts beat as one, their souls entwined in a bond that transcended time and space.

One crisp autumn morning, as the leaves danced in the gentle breeze and the sunlight filtered through the trees, Aarushi and Kabir found themselves standing hand in hand at the edge of a vast meadow. It was a place of quiet beauty, untouched by the passage of time, where the whispers of the wind and the song of the birds filled the air with a sense of peace and tranquility.

As they gazed out across the meadow, their hearts filled with gratitude for the journey they had undertaken together. They had faced trials and tribulations, challenges and obstacles, but through it all, their love had remained unshakable, a beacon of light that had guided them through the darkest of times.

With a sense of reverence, they knelt down on the soft grass, their eyes locked together in a silent exchange of vows. They spoke of their love for each other, of the joys they had shared and the sorrows they had endured, and they pledged to stand by each other's side for all eternity.

As they exchanged rings, a sense of peace washed over them, a peace born from the knowledge that they were exactly where they were meant to be. They knew that the road ahead would not always be easy, that there would be challenges and obstacles to overcome, but they also knew that as long as they had each other, they could face anything that came their way with courage and grace.

With tears of joy in their eyes, they sealed their vows with a kiss, their hearts overflowing with love and gratitude. And as they stood up and turned to face the world together, they knew that their journey was far from over, that their love would continue to grow and evolve with each passing day.

As they walked hand in hand through the meadow, their hearts filled with hope and anticipation for the future, they knew that no matter what challenges lay ahead, they would face them together, with love as their guiding light and each other as their constant companion.

And so, with hearts full of love and eyes shining bright, Aarushi and Kabir embarked on the next chapter of their journey, ready to embrace whatever the future had in store with open arms.

Part 2: The Promise of Forever

As Aarushi and Kabir continued their journey into the depths of their love, they found themselves confronted with the fragility of life and the beauty of the moments they shared. Each day became a celebration of their bond, a testament to the enduring power of their love.

One evening, as they sat beneath a blanket of stars, their hearts filled with gratitude for the love they shared, they found themselves reflecting on the journey that had brought them to this moment. They spoke of the trials they had faced and the obstacles they had overcome, but above all, they spoke of the love that had carried them through it all.

With a sense of reverence, they made a vow to cherish each moment they shared, to savor the sweetness of their love and to hold each other close, no matter what the future held. They promised to stand by each other's side through thick and thin, to support each other through the trials of life, and to celebrate each victory, no matter how small.

As they looked up at the stars twinkling in the night sky, they felt a sense of peace settle over them, a peace born from the knowledge that they were exactly where they were meant to be. Hand in hand, they watched as the stars danced above them, their hearts filled with love and gratitude for the journey they had undertaken together.

And as they drifted off to sleep beneath the canopy of stars, they knew that no matter what challenges lay ahead, they would face them together, with love as their guiding light and each other as their constant companion. And as they dreamed of the adventures that lay ahead, their souls ablaze with the promise of a future filled with boundless possibilities, they knew that their love would endure for all eternity.

And so, with hearts full of hope and eyes shining bright, Aarushi and Kabir embarked on the next chapter of their journey, ready to embrace whatever the future had in store.

Part 3: Embracing the Unknown

As Aarushi and Kabir delved deeper into the essence of their love, they found themselves on the threshold of the unknown, ready to embark on a new chapter of their journey. With each step forward, they embraced the uncertainty of the future, knowing that their love would guide them through whatever challenges lay ahead.

One morning, as they stood on the shores of a vast ocean, the salty breeze caressing their skin and the waves crashing against the shore, they felt a sense of awe wash over them. The ocean stretched out before them, endless and unfathomable, a symbol of the boundless possibilities that lay ahead.

With a sense of reverence, they waded into the water, their feet sinking into the soft sand beneath them. As they swam further out to sea, they felt a sense of liberation wash over them, a freedom born from the knowledge that they were no longer bound by the constraints of the past.

As they floated on the surface of the water, their bodies buoyed by the gentle currents, they reflected on the journey they had undertaken together. They spoke of the challenges they had faced and the obstacles they had overcome, but above all, they spoke of the love that had carried them through it all.

With each passing moment, they felt their bond grow stronger, their souls intertwining in a dance as old as time itself. They knew that the road ahead would not always be easy, that there would be trials and tribulations to overcome, but they also knew that as long as they had each other, they could face anything that came their way with courage and grace.

As they emerged from the water, their bodies refreshed and their spirits renewed, they knew that they were ready to embrace whatever the future held. With hearts full of love and eyes shining bright, they looked to the horizon with hope and anticipation, knowing that their love would guide them through whatever challenges lay ahead.

And as they walked hand in hand along the shore, their footsteps leaving imprints in the sand behind them, they knew that no matter what the future held, they would face it together, with love as their guiding light and each other as their constant companion.

And so, with hearts full of hope and souls ablaze with the promise of a future filled with boundless possibilities, Aarushi and Kabir embarked on the next chapter of their journey, ready to embrace whatever the universe had in store.

Part 4: The Journey Continues

As Aarushi and Kabir stood on the cusp of a new chapter in their lives, they felt a sense of excitement and anticipation coursing through their veins. The journey they had undertaken together had brought them to this moment, where they stood ready to face whatever the future held with courage and determination.

With a renewed sense of purpose, they set out on the road ahead, their hearts filled with love and their souls ablaze with the promise of a future filled with endless possibilities. They knew that the path would not always be easy, that there would be challenges and obstacles to overcome, but they also knew that as long as they had each other, they could overcome anything.

As they traveled through the verdant countryside, their spirits lifted by the beauty of the world around them, they found themselves reflecting on the love that had brought them together. They spoke of the moments they had shared, the laughter and tears, the highs and lows, and they marveled at the depth of their connection.

With each passing mile, they felt their bond grow stronger, their love deepening with every beat of their hearts. They knew that they were meant to be together, that their souls were intertwined in a dance as old as time itself, and they embraced the knowledge with open arms.

As they reached their destination, a small village nestled among the hills, they felt a sense of peace settle over them, a peace born from the knowledge that they were exactly where they were meant to be. Hand in hand, they walked through the streets, their hearts filled with gratitude for the journey they had undertaken together.

And as they looked to the future with hope and anticipation, they knew that their love would guide them through whatever challenges lay ahead. With hearts full of love and eyes shining bright, they embraced the next chapter of their journey with open arms, ready to face whatever the universe had in store.

And so, with hearts full of hope and souls ablaze with the promise of a future filled with boundless possibilities, Aarushi and Kabir embarked on the next chapter of their journey, hand in hand, together forever.

Conclusion: Twisted Love; Horizons

In the culmination of their journey, Aarushi and Kabir stood at the edge of the horizon, where the sky met the earth in an infinite embrace. Their love had weathered storms and soared to great heights, forging a bond that transcended time and space.

As they looked out at the vast expanse before them, they knew that their journey was far from over. With each step, they had embraced the unknown, facing challenges head-on and emerging stronger than before. Their love had been tested, but it had endured, a beacon of hope in a world filled with uncertainty.

In the quiet moments between them, they found solace in each other's arms, knowing that no matter what the future held, they would face it together. Their love was a force to be reckoned with, a source of strength and courage that knew no bounds.

As they stood on the threshold of a new beginning, they felt a sense of peace settle over them, a peace born from the knowledge that they were exactly where they were meant to be. Hand in hand, they embraced the future with open arms, ready to embark on the next chapter of their journey, together.

And as they walked hand in hand into the sunset, their hearts filled with love and gratitude for the journey they had undertaken together, they knew that their love would endure for all eternity, a testament to the power of love to conquer all.

In the end, theirs was a love story for the ages, a tale of passion and perseverance, of trials and triumphs. And as they disappeared into the horizon, their love shone bright, a guiding light for all who dared to dream of a love that knew no bounds.

And so, as the sun dipped below the horizon, casting a warm glow over the world, Aarushi and Kabir walked into the future, their hearts full of hope and their souls ablaze with the promise of a love that would stand the test of time.

About the Author

Mrigendra Bharti, born on June 29, 2004, in South Delhi, India, is a multifaceted individual recognized as the owner of Mrigendra Bharti Group InfoTech India Co. Pvt Ltd. Beyond his entrepreneurial endeavors, he is a distinguished music producer, director, and a budding writer.

Embarking on his professional journey at a young age, Mrigendra Bharti's visionary leadership has led to the establishment of several successful ventures, including Croma Music Series Entertainment, Sellbrochure, Fauget Innovative, and more.

What sets Mrigendra apart is his early initiation into the world of business. His foray into the unknown realms of entrepreneurship began during his 10th-grade years, where he delved into the music industry. This initial venture laid the foundation for subsequent achievements, showcasing his dedication and resilience.

Having honed his skills in music, Mrigendra Bharti not only demonstrated significant growth in his craft but also expanded his professional network. His passion extends beyond music, encompassing app and website development, as well as graphic design.

Fueled by his creative aspirations, Mrigendra established the Mrigendra Bharti Group, a company specializing in website and app development. Currently, he collaborates with a dedicated team, collectively working on ambitious projects that promise innovation and excellence.

Mrigendra's journey serves as an inspiration, particularly for today's students, highlighting the potential of youthful determination and the ability to transform innovative ideas into successful businesses. As he continues to make strides in various domains, Mrigendra Bharti remains a dynamic force, contributing vibrancy to the realms of business, music, and technology.

Read more at https://www.imwriter-mrigendra.rf.gd.

www.ingramcontent.com/pod-product-compliance
Lightning Source LLC
Chambersburg PA
CBHW070823170726
48000CB00019B/2438